THE LITTLE PENGUIN

Chris McEwan

DOUBLEDAY

NEW YORK LONDON TORONTO SYDNEY AUCKLAND

This book belongs to . . .

_____

_____

_____

Published by Doubleday, a division of
Bantam Doubleday Dell Publishing Group, Inc.
666 Fifth Avenue, New York, New York 10103
Published by arrangement with William Collins Sons & Co. Ltd

Doubleday and the portrayal of an anchor with a dolphin
are trademarks of Doubleday, a division of
Bantam Doubleday Dell Publishing Group, Inc.

Library of Congress Cataloging-in-Publication Data
McEwan, Chris.
The little penguin / by Chris McEwan.—1st ed. in the U.S.A.
p.   cm.
Summary: When none of the toy shop toys seems special enough for
the baby prince's royal birthday party present, Little Penguin
decides to give his own special tune and begins a search for Santa
Claus to help him wrap it.
ISBN 0-385-24977-2; ISBN 0-385-24978-0 (lib. bdg.)
[1. Christmas—Fiction.   2. Penguins—Fiction.]   I. Title.
PZ7.M4784544Li   1989
[E]—dc19   88-28655
CIP
AC

Once upon a time, far away in a cold and snowy land, a Baby Prince was born to the King and Queen of the Penguins. So great was their joy that a grand royal birthday party was planned to celebrate the event. This is the story of one Little Penguin who went to that party.

"Special delivery!" announced the postman as he handed an important-looking letter to the Little Penguin.

"It's from the palace!" he cried. "An invitation to a birthday party for the Baby Prince!"

All his friends also had invitations. Now they must each find a present to take to the party.

"Perhaps he would like one of my old toys?" said the Little Penguin.
But it was decided that a visit to the toyshop would be a much better
idea. Then he could choose something really special.

The shop was full of every kind of toy that the Little Penguin could imagine.

But somehow none of them seemed quite special enough for a Baby Prince.

The Little Penguin was worried as he went to bed that night. He tried very hard to think of a really special idea for a birthday present, and as he thought he whistled to himself. He always whistled the same little tune whenever he needed to think.

Suddenly he had the answer.

He would give the Baby Prince his tune!

The Little Penguin frowned. "But however will I wrap it up? Oh dear."

All at once the room was filled with an amazing light.

Out of the shining light there appeared a Fairy Penguin.
"Permit me to help you, if I can," she said kindly. "I know a place where
we will surely find the answer to your problem. Come with me. Come."
And together they flew out of the bedroom window and off into the
night sky.

Onward they flew – faster and higher over mountains and seas – until at last they landed – PLOP – in deep soft snow.

"Where are we?" asked the Little Penguin.
"These are the North Lands," said a passing snowman, "home of the Winter King."

"We must go in search of Santa Claus," said the Fairy Penguin. "He knows everything about wrapping gifts."

Some friendly bears showed them the way. They wandered through the icy corridors guarded by snobots. Down freezing stairways and across chilly chambers they strayed, until at last they found themselves in the awesome presence of a vast and frosty giant.

The Little Penguin was rather shy, but his fairy friend boldly explained that they were trying to find Santa Claus to ask for his help in making a parcel of the Little Penguin's tune.

"I am Jack Frost!" the icy giant roared in a voice like the north wind.
"Give *me* your tune and I will turn it to splinters of ice. I will wrap it in hoarfrost and seal it with freezing flakes of snow!"

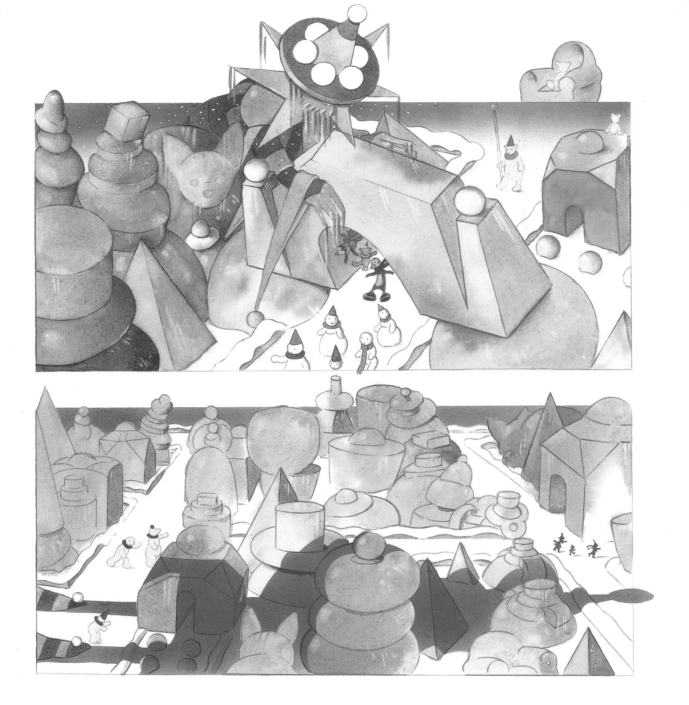

"Thank you," said the Fairy Penguin politely, "but that wouldn't do at all, for how would we ever unwrap such a parcel? If you would be so kind as to show us the way, we will see what Santa Claus has to say." There was a long chilly silence while Jack Frost stared at the two friends, then he said coldly, "Come, I will show you the path that leads into my garden." Then he laughed loudly. "But you will have to find your own way out!"

The ice garden seemed to go on forever, and around them the sound of Jack Frost's laughter echoed like a raging blizzard. All was well, however, for warm, friendly faces soon began to appear.

Together they journeyed to the gates of Christmas Land, where more friends waited to greet them.
"We are Santa Claus's helpers. How may we help you?"

"We would like to see Santa Claus, please," said the Fairy Penguin.
"I need his help to wrap a present," announced the Little Penguin.
Everyone was very surprised at this.
"He is *awfully* busy, you know," said one robot sternly. Suddenly they
heard a sound and turned to see a huge door slowly opening…

Behind the door was Santa Claus himself!
He took the friends to his parlor and over tea the Little Penguin told him
all about the Baby Prince's birthday present. When the story was
finished and the Little Penguin had whistled his tune, Santa Claus
nodded wisely.
"Bravo!" he cried. "That will be an excellent gift, but it is not an easy
task, to put a tune into a parcel."

They took the problem to the workshops and, after instructions from
Santa Claus, buttons were pressed, switches switched, levers pulled,
workers worked, and helpers helped. Finally, a long time later,
a beautifully wrapped parcel tied with ribbon emerged from a machine
and was presented to the Little Penguin.

"Come quickly," said the Fairy Penguin. "It is time to leave. The party is tomorrow and today is almost yesterday. We mustn't be late!"
Home they flew with the precious parcel, tumbling and falling through the air, until at last the Little Penguin found himself crash-landing on his own familiar bed!

The Little Penguin's parents were amazed when they heard about Santa Claus's workshops and how the tune was put into the parcel. Before long he was tucked up in bed where, thinking happily about tomorrow's party, he soon fell into a deep sleep.

It was the day of the Baby Prince's party!
Everyone dressed in their party clothes and set off for the palace.
On skis and snowshoes, sleds and skates they went, and the last to arrive
was the Fairy Penguin.

All the guests presented their gifts to the Baby Prince, until finally it was the turn of the Little Penguin.

"The Prince is very glum," said the King, looking worried. "If your gift doesn't make him smile, then the party will be canceled and everyone must go home."

The Little Penguin bowed and placed his parcel on the royal cradle. The baby frowned even harder, then pulled the ribbon with all his might.

The wrapping fell open.
Inside was a box.
Then a lid flew up and music filled the air! Inside the box a tiny fairy
penguin twirled round and round in time to the Little Penguin's happy
tune.

Soon the band began to play along with the melody. The Baby Prince started to smile and the more the music played the wider his smile became.
Everyone danced including the King and Queen, while the Baby Prince laughed and laughed!

It was the best party that anyone could remember.

The baby was still smiling as they said their goodbyes. The two friends flew home, but the Fairy Penguin stopped at the garden gate.

"I must leave now," she said. "There is much to be done," and she flew off into the night.

"But when will I see you again?" called the Little Penguin. The answer came back faintly from the darkness,

"Whenever you look for me."

"The only thing is," sighed the Little Penguin, "once my tune was put into a box, I found I couldn't remember it at all! How will I do any serious thinking without my tune?"

Just then the doorbell rang, and there on the step, softly playing the Little Penguin's tune, was another music box! Far above a tiny light flickered once before fading away in the night sky.

· THE END ·